First published in Great Britain in 2010 by
Random House Books
Random House, 20 Vauxhall Bridge Road,
London SW1V 2SA

www.rbooks.co.uk

The Random House Group Limited Reg. No. 954009

ISBN : 9780099544241

2 4 6 8 10 9 7 5 3 1

Design: Dynamo Limited
Text: Kay Wilkins
Interior Artwork: Ailin Chambers

Printed and bound in Great Britain by CPI Bookmarque, Croydon

The Random House Group Limited supports The Forest Stewardship
Council (FSC), the leading international forest certification organisation.
All our titles that are printed on Greenpeace approved FSC certified paper
carry the FSC logo. Our paper procurement policy can be found at:
www.rbooks.co.uk/environment

THE DRAGON'S TRIANGLE

PUBLISHING

a Jim Pattison Company

INTRODUCING THE RBI

Hidden away on a small island off the East Coast of the United States is Ripley High – a unique school for children who possess extraordinary talents.

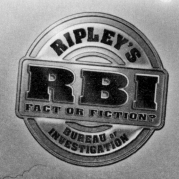

Located in the former home of Robert Ripley – creator of the world-famous Ripley's Believe It or Not! – the school takes students who all share a secret. Although they look like you or me, they have amazing skills: the ability to conduct electricity, superhuman strength, or control over the weather – these are just a few of the talents the Ripley High School students possess.

The very best of these talented kids have been invited to join a top secret agency – Ripley's Bureau of Investigation: the RBI. This elite group operates from a hi-tech underground base hidden deep beneath the school. From here, the talented teen agents are sent on dangerous missions around the world, investigating sightings of fantastical creatures and strange occurrences. Join them on their incredible adventures as they seek out the weird and the wonderful, and try to separate fact from fiction ...

RIPLEY

The Department of Unbelievable Lies

A mysterious rival agency determined to stop the RBI and discredit Ripley's by sabotaging the Ripley's database

The spirit of Robert Ripley lives on in RIPLEY, a supercomputer that stores the database – all Ripley's bizarre collections, and information on all the artefacts and amazing discoveries made by the RBI. Featuring a fully interactive holographic Ripley as its interface, RIPLEY gives the agents info on their missions and sends them invaluable data on their R-phones.

THE TEACHERS

Mr Cain

The agents' favourite teacher, Mr Cain, runs the RBI – under the guise of a Museum Club – and coordinates all the agents' missions.

Dr Maxwell

The only other teacher at the school who knows about the RBI. Dr Maxwell equips the agents for their missions with cutting-edge gadgets from his lab.

MEET THE RBI TEAM

As well as having amazing talents, each of the seven members of the RBI has expert knowledge in their own individual fields of interest. All with different skills, the team supports each other at school and while out on missions, where the three most suitable agents are chosen for each case.

The RBI team keep in touch with each other, while on missions, using their R-phones. They also receive facts and useful information from RIPLEY in this way.

▶▶ KOBE

NAME : Kobe Shakur

AGE : 15

SKILLS : Excellent tracking and endurance skills, tribal knowledge and telepathic abilities

NOTES : Kobe's parents grew up in different African tribes. Kobe has amazing tracking capabilities and is an expert on native cultures across the world. He can also tell the entire history of a person or object just by touching it.

▶▶ ZIA

NAME : Zia Mendoza

AGE : 13

SKILLS : Possesses magnetic and electrical powers. Can predict the weather

NOTES : The only survivor of a tropical storm that destroyed her village when she was a baby. Zia doesn't yet fully understand her abilities but she can predict and sometimes control the weather. Her presence can also affect electrical equipment.

▶▶ MAX

NAME : Max Johnson

AGE : 14

SKILLS : Computer genius and inventor

NOTES : Max, from Las Vegas, loves computer games and anything electrical. He spends most of his spare time inventing robots. Max hates school but he loves spending time helping Dr Maxwell come up with new gadgets.

▶▶ KATE

NAME : Kate Jones

AGE : 14

SKILLS : Computer-like memory, extremely clever and ability to master languages in minutes

NOTES : Raised at Oxford University in England by her history professor and part-time archaeologist uncle, Kate memorised every book in the University library after reading them only once!

▶▶ ALEK

NAME : Alek Filipov

AGE : 15

SKILL : Contortionist with amazing physical strength

NOTES : Alek is a member of the Russian under-16 Olympic gymnastics team and loves sports and competitions. He is much bigger than the other agents, and although he seems quiet and serious much of the time, he has a wicked sense of humour.

▶▶ LI

NAME : Li Yong

AGE : 15

SKILL : Musical genius with pitch-perfect hearing and the ability to mimic any sound

NOTES : Li grew up in a wealthy family in Beijing, China, and joined Ripley High later than the other RBI agents. She has a highly developed sense of hearing and can imitate any sound she hears.

▶▶ JACK

NAME : Jack Stevens

AGE : 14

SKILLS : Can 'talk' to animals and has expert survival skills

NOTES : Jack grew up on an animal park in the Australian outback. He has always shared a strong bond with animals and can communicate with any creature – and loves to eat weird food!

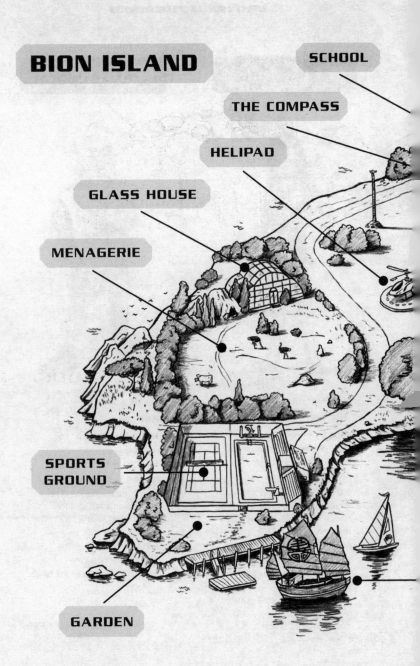

BION ISLAND

SCHOOL

THE COMPASS

HELIPAD

GLASS HOUSE

MENAGERIE

SPORTS
GROUND

GARDEN

CHINESE GARDEN

STONE MONUMENT (Secret Entrance)

WATER ENTRANCE TO SECRET CAVE

SECRET RBI LAB

DOCKS

MON LEI

Prologue

"Isn't it beautiful, Riki?" Aimi asked, as she watched the sun sink lower over the North Pacific Ocean.

"It would be better if that mist cleared," said Riki. He had been so pleased with his idea to take Aimi to see the sunset, hoping she would find it really romantic. Now the two of them were sitting in his car and a sea mist had appeared out of nowhere, hiding the setting sun behind it.

"But don't you think it's amazing, the way the sun is so bright that it's burning through all that horrible mist?" asked Aimi. "It's like a glowing ruby, smouldering its way through an enchanted smog."

Riki frowned at his girlfriend's poetic description and looked carefully, trying to see what she meant; he did see a glowing ruby, two of them in fact. Twin spheres of red light were blazing through the mist, and they seemed to be moving.

"I don't think that's the sun," he said, peering ahead to make out the source of the lights. They were too close together for car headlights but they were definitely moving towards them. "Maybe we should come back tomorrow?"

Riki could see the disappointment on Aimi's face as she stared out into the haze; but then her expression changed to one of fear. He looked out of the window as she let out a piercing scream; a dark shape was emerging from the fog. Riki couldn't make out what it was, but the glowing red lights were definitely eyes. In a panic, he turned the ignition key, but the engine wouldn't start.

"What's wrong?" asked Aimi. "Why won't it start?"

Riki silently cursed his old car. The sea mist was affecting the ancient engine.

"Riki, I want to go," Aimi pleaded.

"I think we need to run," he told her, throwing open the car door. Aimi did the same, and Riki ran around the car and grabbed her hand. He pulled her with him as he ran away from the car and the strange creature closing in on it.

Only seconds later, Riki felt a blast of hot air scorch his back and neck. Aimi tripped and fell and as he bent down to help her up, he turned back to see the source of the heat. The huge dark shape was now right where they had been. Flames were streaming from its mouth and Riki's car had been consumed in a giant ball of flames.

Auto-Alek

"Dr Maxwell, you have to see this – it's amazing," said Max, rushing through the door to the technology lab. He had just finished a geography lesson and had run at top speed to show his favourite professor his new invention.

"Hello, Max," said Dr Maxwell, taken aback by the sudden entrance.

"I worked on it all weekend," Max explained, as he set his project up. It was a small, shining metal man leaning over a golf club, ready to swing. "It's a golfing robot," he added.

"You were supposed to wait for me," said Alek, as he came through the door just behind his excited friend. "I helped you with it, after all."

"He did help," Max agreed. "I don't know a lot about golf, so I studied Alek's movements as he putted some balls and I replicated them here." He gestured to the robot that was now on the desk.

▶▶ Each year the RoboGames is held in San Francisco, with robots from all over the world competing in 70 different events, including golf, fighting, basketball, weightlifting, soccer and even robot sumo. You can watch 150-kilogramme robots shooting flames or cartwheeling down a soccer field!

"I put the little pot here," said Max, placing a small pot a little way along the table from the robot.

"And I place the golf ball here," said Alek, putting the ball down in front of the odd-looking contraption.

"Then I turn it on," said Max, flicking the on/off switch, "and hey presto!"

The robot wiggled its golf club as if it was judging the distance to the pot, rocked the club into a backswing and then brought it forward to hit the ball. The amount of pressure was just enough to putt the ball perfectly into the pot.

"That's brilliant!" said Dr Maxwell, clapping his hands together in admiration.

"What is?" asked Jack. He had heard his friends' voices in the technology lab and wandered in.

"Max has a new robot," Alek told him. "That I helped him build."

"Set it up again," called out one of the other students. Max looked up to see that quite a crowd had followed Jack in.

"Okay," he smiled, pleased that his robot was proving to be such a big hit. "I'll put the cup back."

"I place the golf ball," said Alek, keen to show that he was part of this experiment too, "and Max switches the Auto-Alek on –"

Max turned to look at his friend in surprise. "The Auto-Alek?" he asked.

"Oh," said Alek, embarrassed. "As it was based on me, I thought you might call it that."

Max smiled at him.

"But you don't have to," Alek added quickly.

"No, I think the Auto-Alek sounds great," Max said. Alek beamed.

"So, I switch on the Auto-Alek," Max continued, "and ..."

This time, the little robot judged the distance to the pot, but then pulled its golf club back with a jerk and took an almighty swing, firing the golf ball over the pot and straight through the glass window. It then started hacking at the table with its golf club. Splinters of wood flew up into the air and Max, Alek and Dr Maxwell had to jump back quickly. The robot swung its club wildly, hitting anything in sight, and then spun around in a circle, lost its balance and tipped over, crashing onto the destroyed table its club still swinging at the air.

A loud intake of breath sounded from the stunned audience, followed by a stony silence, which Dr Maxwell broke.

"Yes, well, maybe there are still a few bugs to

work out," he suggested, looking at his broken window.

"No, no, there aren't," argued Max. "The 'Auto-Alek' always works perfectly!"

"I don't think that's a good name for it anymore," said Alek quickly.

"Er, I hate to argue with you, mate," said Jack, as he grabbed a dustpan and brush and

started sweeping up shards of window. "But I wouldn't call that perfect – unless you meant to destroy the lab, of course." Had it been Mr Willis's classroom, Jack would have been certain that it was exactly what Max had meant to do, as Max had a very strong rebellious streak. However, the technology lab was another story. Max was gifted when it came to creating and understanding machines, and he spent hours there outside school time, working on his various projects.

"I just don't understand ..." Max frowned, staring at the Auto-Alek that was now on its back on the table, with its feet waving in the air and its club still swinging in its hand. He looked up from the suffering robot to where Jack was clearing up when something caught his eye.

"Wait a minute..." said Max, as he watched a figure move through the crowd towards the door – a figure with a silver streak in otherwise black hair. "Oh, Zia?" he called. Zia winced at having been seen. "Have you been here long, Z?"

"Hmm?" said Zia, turning around and pretending she didn't know anything.

"Zia," said Max, starting to sound angry.

"Oh, okay," said Zia. "I just wanted to see what everyone was looking at. And then I was interested to see how the robot worked. I thought if I stood at the back, it wouldn't make any difference."

"Well, you were wrong, weren't you?" asked Max, cross that Zia had disrupted his demonstration. Her ability allowed her to predict, and even control, the weather as she was in tune with the electromagnetism in the air. Sometimes, however, her magnetic vibes made electrical equipment go a little crazy.

"I'm sorry," Zia apologised. "I'm sorry about your lab too, Dr Maxwell, especially the window."

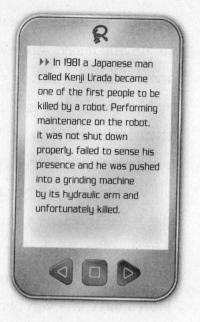

▶▶ In 1981 a Japanese man called Kenji Urada became one of the first people to be killed by a robot. Performing maintenance on the robot, it was not shut down properly, failed to sense his presence and he was pushed into a grinding machine by its hydraulic arm and unfortunately killed.

"It will be fine, Zia," Dr Maxwell assured her. "Max, your robot will be fine too. Just let it recover for a bit and the Auto-Alek – sorry, Alek – the robot will be as good as new."

"So it will work again?" asked Alek.

"I should think so," said Dr Maxwell.

"Then I think the Auto-Alek is a good name for the robot," Alek decided.

Jack was about to comment on Alek's constant name changes when his R-phone buzzed in his pocket.

"Ooh, Museum Club," he announced, as he

read his message. "We've got a meeting, right now – and it says 'hope you like sushi'. I wonder what that means?"

Mr Cain often gave them cryptic clues to their latest mission.

"Then go," said Dr Maxwell. "I'll clear up here." He looked at Zia, who still had a guilty look on her face. "It wasn't your fault, Zia," he tried to reassure her. "To be honest, I've been trying to get some new equipment for the lab for a while. Now I have an even better reason for needing some funding. That window needed cleaning too, it will save me having to ask Mr Clarkson to do it!"

Zia smiled at her teacher's joke and followed the others out of the lab.

2

Monster and Machine

"Oh, no – Mr Clarkson," whispered Max, diving behind an open door. "Man, what's he doing here now?"

Mr Clarkson was the Ripley High caretaker, and the agents were always a little suspicious of his interest in what they were doing. They even wondered if he might be working for DUL, the rival agency who was always trying to cause trouble. Right now, Mr Clarkson was cleaning

the statue that activated the secret entrance
to the RBI lab.

"He's dusting Liu Min
again!" Max complained.

"He's always cleaning
one of those heads," said
Kate. "I think he's seen us
all hanging around here
and is wondering why."

"What should we do?"
asked Zia as she watched
the caretaker carefully
studying the head he was
polishing. "If we're not
careful he'll look straight
into Liu Min's eye and set
off the secret retina scan!"

"His eye-print isn't
logged as belonging to a member of the RBI,
so it shouldn't open the door," said Kate. "But
I'll try to get him to clean somewhere else, just

in case." She walked up to the caretaker and put
on her sweetest smile.

"Good morning, Mr
Clarkson," she greeted
him innocently. "Gosh,
those heads are really
gleaming."

"No, I found some 'bad
show'," he told her. 'Bad
show' was his term for
anything that was wrong
in the school. He thought
of Ripley High as a giant
'showcase' – which in
some ways it was – and he
couldn't stand anything
that wasn't show-worthy.
"There is something on
this one that I just can't get off. I saw that
American boy hanging around yesterday. It's
probably some of that awful gum he chews."

"Hey, why me?" protested Max from his hiding place.

Jack 'shushed' him quickly.

"It looks fine to me," Kate offered.

"No, no, it's still 'bad show'," he insisted.

"Mr Clarkson, come quickly!" Li arrived beside Kate, out of breath. "I've just come from the East Wing and there are some boys swinging from the bubblegum chandelier outside the Maths room."

"The scoundrels!" exclaimed Mr Clarkson, running off quickly to investigate the disturbance. "That is most definitely 'bad show'!"

▶▶Ya Ya Chou from California, USA, made a chandelier by stringing hundreds of different flavoured Gummi bears together with beads and string.

▶▶ Mexican-Brazilian artist Carolina Fontoura creates light shades and chandeliers from old bike wheels, gear cogs and chains.

"Are there really boys swinging from that

chandelier?" asked Kate, when Mr Clarkson had gone.

"Not unless Max has somehow teleported himself there from behind that door," said Li, catching her breath.

"Hey, why me?" asked Max again. "Although that does sound like fun!"

Kate groaned at Max's immaturity as they all filed down into the RBI headquarters.

"Oh, good. You're all here," said Mr Cain. The agents took their seats around the big meeting table. "We have a 'double mission'. We have received reports from Japan of a huge dragon attacking people."

"Like a Komodo dragon?" asked Jack.

"No, I don't think so," said Mr Cain. "RIPLEY?"

The holographic representation of the Ripley database appeared.

"Hello, agents," he said.

"Hi, RIPLEY," they all replied.

A grainy image appeared on the large view screen. The picture was very misty, but the agents could make out a dark shape and a pair of glowing red eyes. At the bottom of the picture they could just see a car, but it looked as if something was pressing down on the roof.

"Is that a foot?" asked Kate.

"Well, that's definitely not a Komodo dragon," said Jack.

"Believe it or not, we've received several sightings of this dragon," RIPLEY explained.

"It appears at a particular place along the coast, near Tokyo, and is usually accompanied by all that sea mist that you can see."

"Oh! That's sea mist," said Max. "I thought Zia had just got close to the camera!"

"Be nice, Max," warned Mr Cain. Zia stuck her tongue out at Max.

"The mists are in keeping with the local folklore about mythical dragons who were supposed to live in the nearby seas," RIPLEY continued. "So your mission is to investigate the dragon and see if it qualifies for entry into the database."

"The other part of your mission," Mr Cain took over, "is to go and see a local inventor, named Ren Nagano."

"Ren is someone we have had on our list of people to contact for quite a while," said RIPLEY. "He refers to himself as a 'scrapyard scientist' and his latest creation is a robot that does tricks on his command. He thinks we should enter it into the database."

"Max, you will be going to Japan as our resident robot expert," said Mr Cain. "Alek, you will also be going to assess the robot's strength, and Zia, you will be the third member. If the dragon appears only when there is a sea mist, you might be able to get to the bottom of why that is."

The agents all nodded their agreement.

"Oh, and we're having a fundraiser this weekend," Mr Cain added.

"What for?" asked Kobe.

"I hear Dr Maxwell needs a new lab," Mr Cain told them, smiling.

"Ouch, that was bad," groaned Max as he left.

3

Dragons and Disappearances

While Max returned to see Dr Maxwell and find out what gadgets he could give them for this mission, Zia and Alek went to see Miss Burrows, the agents' geography teacher. Like all the other 'regular' teachers in the school, she knew nothing about the RBI.

"Let's pretend that we're doing a project on Japanese dragon myths," suggested Zia.

"Well, we are ... kind of," said Alek.

"There are lots of Japanese myths about dragons," Miss Burrows told them in response to their enquiry. "Any particular one you have in mind?"

"How about around the Tokyo area?" Alek asked.

"Ooh, then you'll want to know about the Dragon's Triangle," she told them.

"What's that?" asked Zia.

"Have you heard of the Bermuda Triangle?" Miss Burrows asked them.

"Isn't that an area of the ocean where lots of planes and ships have vanished?" asked Alek.

"A point to the Russian gymnast," replied Miss Burrows enthusiastically.

"There are a lot of tropical storms in that area," offered Zia. "It's sometimes suggested that the weather is responsible for many of the disappearances."

"Right again," Miss Burrows nodded. "Other possible explanations include aliens abducting people. However, one theory is that it is related to the Earth's magnetic fields."

"Hey, it wasn't me, honest!" smiled Zia.

"Thank goodness Max isn't here," said Alek. "He would be blaming you."

"I don't think it's anything to do with you, Zia," Miss Burrows laughed. "However, it is linked to the same electromagnetic signals that you are tuned in to. You both know that a compass always points north, don't you?"

Both the agents nodded.

"Well, it actually points to magnetic north," Miss Burrows continued. "True north can be anything up to 20 degrees away in either direction, depending where you are in the world."

Alek looked confused.

"The reasons why don't really matter here," said Miss Burrows. "Just trust me on it. In the Bermuda Triangle, true north and magnetic north are one and the same. So the theory goes that this overlap causes the static and interference that pilots hear on their radios in the Bermuda Triangle."

"Like when Zia gets too close to my MP3 player," said Alek, understanding. "But what does this have to do with Japan?"

"Ah, well, there is one other place on earth where true north and magnetic north are the same," Miss Burrows told them. "It's called the Dragon's Triangle. It starts north of Tokyo, comes down past the Bonin Islands until it reaches Guam and the island of Yap." She drew a line on her large map of the world. "There, it turns and goes straight across to Taiwan, before turning again and coming back up to include the Bay of Tokyo."

▶▶ In the area of ocean known as the Dragon's Triangle, strange disappearances have been reported. Legends tell of restless dragons rising from the depths and dragging ships back to their underground watery homes. In 1952 a Japanese boat with 31 crew on board was sent to investigate but it never returned. The mystery remains unsolved!

The agents looked at the world map and saw that their teacher had drawn a triangle.

"Have there been disappearances in the Dragon's Triangle, too?" asked Alek.

"There certainly have been," Miss Burrows replied. "The most famous one is Amelia Earhart, who might have vanished in the Dragon's Triangle."

"Who's Amelia Earhart?" asked Alek.

"She was a famous pilot, the first woman to fly across the Atlantic," explained Zia. "So, why is it called the Dragon's Triangle? Why not the Pacific Triangle?"

"I was hoping you'd ask that," said Miss Burrows. "A Chinese myth says that the disappearances of the people, ships and planes in that area are down to dragons who live beneath the waves. They surface only when they are angered. They can also churn up whirlpools and change the weather, so that a clear day can become shrouded in mist."

▶▶ Scientists at Britain's Natural History Museum could hardly believe their eyes in 2003 when confronted with a baby dragon, preserved in a jar of formaldehyde. The dragon had been discovered during a garage clear-out in Oxfordshire. It emerged later that the dragon was a forgery - a modern hoax!

Zia and Alek looked at each other. That would explain the

sea spray that hung in the air whenever the dragon they were to investigate was sighted.

"Most Japanese don't believe that, though," Miss Burrows continued. "They don't believe that the waters off the coast of Tokyo are any more dangerous than anywhere else along their shoreline."

"I bet they do now," said Alek quietly, as he and Zia thanked their teacher for the information and headed off to 'write up' their research.

"Look what Dr Maxwell gave us," said Max, as he walked into the RBI base where Zia and Alek were looking at maps. He was wearing a state-of-the-art fireproof vest. It looked similar to the bulletproof vests that police officers wear, but was made of a fireproof material that wouldn't heat up and cook the agents. "I feel like a medieval knight," he announced, lunging at Alek and pretending to swipe with an imaginary sword.

Zia picked up one of the other vests that Max had put on the table.

"Ooh, they're really light too," she said. "I thought it was going to feel like a real suit of armour!"

"That's not all," Max told them, pulling out another gadget that looked like a larger version of their R-phones, but boxier and with added buttons and antennae.

"It's a fish finder," said Alek. "I use one of these when I go fishing."

"Close," said Max. "It's a top-of-the-range, handheld sonar device. It's like a fish finder but much more powerful."

"How do these things work?" asked Zia.

"Sonar stands for Sound Navigation and Ranging," Max explained. "It works using sound waves. The small transmitter creates electrical pulses, like small electric shocks. It sends these pulses out as sound waves that travel through the water, or air, until they hit an object. Then they bounce back to the device that then works out the distance to the thing that they hit."

"The same way Li can see where things are in the dark."

"Exactly," said Max. "Li can see in the dark the way bats do. Bats send out signals at different frequencies. They then listen to the echoes and see them as pictures. The echoes tell the bat what is there, how fast it is moving and the direction it is travelling in – that's how they catch moths and stuff. This machine draws a little map for you on the screen. Neither Li nor the bats do that."

"So what are we meant to use this for?" asked Zia.

"Dr Maxwell thought it would be useful for finding things in that sea mist," Max replied.

"Wait a minute," said Zia. "Are we meant to go into the mist after the dragon that crushes cars with its bare foot?"

"If we need to," Max told her.

Zia gulped. She wasn't sure she fancied coming face to face with a 'real' dragon.

Scrapyard Sculptures

Tokyo International Airport was outside the city. As soon as the agents had gone through immigration, they jumped straight on the high-speed bullet train that would take them to the area where the dragon had last been seen. Zia was disappointed that she would not get to see the city, or to visit its museums. She would have loved to have seen the Kaminarimon, or 'Thunder Gate' to give the gate its English name

– the thousand-year-old gate at the entrance to the Senso-ji Temple. But then Zia looked across at Max, who was watching the scenery pass by the window with a mischievous smile on his face.

Tokyo was also famous for its amazing neon lights. Some people even said that the Ginza district rivalled Las Vegas for the amount of bright lights on display. Zia remembered the stories of how Max, who was originally from Las Vegas, would go into the downtown area and wreak havoc, messing about with the lights on the hotels and casinos. Max's amazing computer skills meant that Max could make machines work in

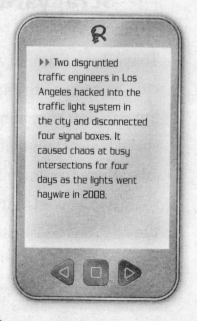

▶▶ Two disgruntled traffic engineers in Los Angeles hacked into the traffic light system in the city and disconnected four signal boxes. It caused chaos at busy intersections for four days as the lights went haywire in 2008.

any way he pleased, and, often, it pleased Max to cause mischief. For example, disrupting the delivery of power to a neon sign so that its display changed. Once, Max transformed one of the biggest billboards on the Las Vegas Strip to say 'Max rules'!

Unfortunately for Max, that had been pretty hard to deny when his mum found out – he'd been grounded for over a month! Yes, Zia decided, it was worth missing Tokyo city centre rather than have to explain to Mr Cain why the San-ai building lights now read 'DUL sucks', or whatever came into Max's head at the time.

"I can see the sea!" shouted Max, as Yokohama Bay came into view.

"We can see the sea every day back on BION Island," said Alek.

"But that's the Atlantic, and this is the Pacific," Max explained. "It's not every day we see the largest ocean in the world."

Soon, the journey was over and the RBI agents stepped off the train.

"Which part of our mission should we investigate first?" asked Zia.

"Let's go see if we can find the dragon," suggested Alek, full of enthusiasm.

"Cool," replied Max, sliding down the sunglasses he usually kept on his head to shield his eyes from the bright sunshine, as they set off for the location of the dragon sightings. There were lots of people there who claimed to have seen the dragon, but most of the reports were a little unclear.

"I was too busy running to see much," one witness told them, "but those horrible red eyes are burned into my memory. Every time I close my eyes I can still see them."

"I tried to get a good look," another explained, "but it was completely surrounded by sea mist. All I could see was the blurry outline of something big and those glowing red eyes."

"I saw it for a split second at sunset," someone else claimed, "but the sunlight reflecting off the creature's scales was blinding. Then the mist appeared and the creature was gone."

The agents tried to piece together all the different clues.

▶▶ The Chinese government sends special aeroplanes into the clouds to make it rain. It tried to guarantee perfect weather for the 2008 Beijing Olympics by firing chemicals into the sky with anti-aircraft guns.

▶▶ The US Air Force flew planes directly into cyclones in the 1960s in an attempt to weaken the storms.

"So, the dragon hardly ever appears without the sea mist," Zia started them off. "That means it must have some way of controlling the weather, or at least water."

"Everyone says that it has red, glowing eyes," said Alek.

"And shiny scales," added Max, "and it is big."

"So we don't really know a lot, do we?" asked Zia.

"Well, in all the reports, people said that they had seen the dragon at sunset or just after dark," said Alek. "That's a start."

"What shall we do now, then?" asked Zia. "It's only half past two."

"I say we start the other half of this mission and see that inventor, then come back here for sunset," suggested Max. Alek and Zia nodded and the three set off to find Ren Nagano and his new invention.

The agents arrived at the address they had been given.

"But this is a scrapyard," complained Alek. "I thought Nagano would work from an amazingly futuristic lab."

"Maybe he doesn't need it," said Zia.

"Or maybe his workshop is here," suggested Max. "It would be a great place to get parts."

Just then, the large gates opened at the front of the yard and a small, wiry man with glasses appeared to greet them.

"Welcome, RBI agents," he said. "I have been so excited about your visit."

Zia smiled; she took an instant liking to Ren Nagano. His English was perfect and he was full of energy – as he walked the agents through his scrapyard and workshop, he almost seemed to bounce.

"I moved my workshop here because of the amazing amount of materials that I could use in my work," he explained.

Max threw a look at the other two agents, making sure they knew that his idea had been right. However, his attention was soon back on Ren when he revealed an astounding line-up of robots and machines made from various tubes, wires, cables and bits of metal.

"Wow, does this robot really change car tyres?" asked Max of one particularly odd-looking machine.

"My mum could use that," said Alek. "She always seems to get flat tyres."

"I built a robot that plays golf," Max announced proudly. "It can putt a ball from a distance of 12 metres."

"Now, I could use that," said Ren.

"What's that?" asked Zia, as they came to an enormous canvas sheet covering something in the corner of the yard.

"Ah, that is my dragon statue, Ryujin," explained Ren. "It's based on the dragon god who rules the seas and represents the power of the ocean. Ryujin lives in an undersea palace and controls the tides with magic jewels. I love robotics, but my other love is dragons. I grew up hearing stories like that, about the dragons that live in the sea just off our coast and was fascinated by them."

"That's weird," said Zia. "We're here to investigate the rumours of dragon sightings not far from here."

"How exciting," he said. "Do you think it is a real dragon, or someone playing a trick?"

"That's what we're here to find out," Zia told him. "Why do you think someone would be playing a trick like that?"

"Because I always imagined that one day I would see a dragon for myself," Ren explained. "As a child I spent hours at the beach hoping one would appear, but it never did. I can't believe that one really exists and I just haven't seen it. Now, I have my very own dragon." Ren pointed to his statue, but then seemed to change his mind. "But we are not here to talk about dragons. There's something else I want to show you."

As Ren led the agents away from the sculpture Max held back; he just couldn't resist a glance at the enormous dragon statue.

"Wow!" he said as he peered under the rough fabric of the cover. From what he could see, the statue had a long, serpentine body that snaked its way along the ground. It seemed to be built from polished steel; as the sun caught the parts Max could see they glinted in the afternoon sun. He could just about make out two strong-looking legs, each with three toes, that seemed to hold the statue up at the front.

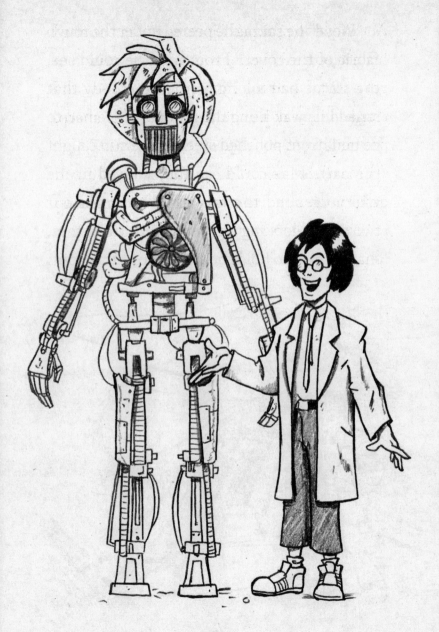

Another two propped up its rear. Max pushed his head further under the tarpaulin, trying to get a glimpse of the dragon's face. If he really craned his neck he could see the tip of sharp, pointed horns above dark, empty eyes.

"Max!" he heard Zia call and quickly and quietly dropped the tarpaulin and tried to rejoin the others without anyone noticing, but Ren saw him.

"Ryujin is just a statue, nothing worthy of the RIPLEY database," he explained. "This, however, is much more impressive."

In front of the agents was a large robot that looked like a huge version of Ren Nagano – it even had his glasses!

5

Electronic Interference

"This is the creation I wanted you to see," said Ren. "I think it deserves a place in your RIPLEY database."

"What does it do?" asked Zia.

"Well, I strap this suit on," he began, pulling a mechanical suit over his clothes, "and then my robot replicates my movements."

The suit was a giant robotic exoskeleton; ankle and kneepads strapped Ren's legs to robotic legs, and his feet slid into metallic shoes at the end of them. A breastplate fastened the top half of the robotic suit to Ren's body, and his gloves allowed him to move the arms. With the suit on, Ren looked even more like a miniature version of his creation.

He began to wave his arms around and the giant robot waved its arms too. Seeing that the agents were impressed, the inventor started dancing around and the robot danced too.

"It's good," said Alek.

"Yes," agreed Max. "But it's not quite RIPLEY-worthy. I've seen robots and technology that do this before."

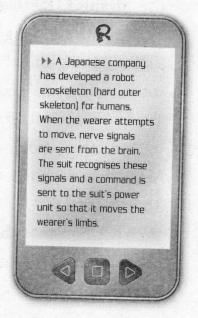

▸▸ A Japanese company has developed a robot exoskeleton (hard outer skeleton) for humans. When the wearer attempts to move, nerve signals are sent from the brain. The suit recognises these signals and a command is sent to the suit's power unit so that it moves the wearer's limbs.

"How does it work, though?" asked Zia. "Does it use infrared beams like a remote control?" She moved closer to the robot to see how it followed what the suit was doing.

Suddenly, the robot started to act strangely. It lurched violently to the side and then its arm shot out in front of it. Its legs began wildly kicking the air, narrowly missing Zia. Alek darted forward and pulled her to safety, out of the robot's kick-zone.

"What is it doing?" asked Alek.

"Look at Ren," said Zia, pointing at the inventor. Ren was flailing around, his movements matching the robot.

"Something must have happened to the robot," said Max, "and it's somehow reversed the flow of the data stream."

The other two agents looked blankly at Max; they found it difficult to follow his 'techno-speak'.

"What I mean is that instead of the robot copying Ren's movements, it is now telling Ren what to do."

"We should help him," suggested Alek as Ren sailed past him, arms and legs waving madly. Alek dashed over to the inventor, trying to hold him still.

"We need to get you out of that suit," Alek shouted.

"I ... can't ... stop it," said Ren, as he tried to catch his breath between scissor kicks and punches. "You ... need to ... stop the robot ... then suit ... stop ... also."

"What?" asked Alek.

"You need to stop the robot!" Max shouted. "Then the suit will stop too."

Alek ran over to the robot. He ducked a punching arm and jumped over a kicking leg, leaping out of the way as the robot suddenly changed direction.

"I'm not sure I can get to it," he said.

"Yes, you can," encouraged Max. "Keep trying."

Alek jumped on the robot's back and, using

his amazing strength, attempted to wrestle it to the ground, but Ren's invention was just too big and strong. It whirled and flung Alek out of the way, as if he was nothing more than a doll.

Zia gasped to see her friend land with a thud across the scrapyard, but Alek quickly stood up, dusted himself off and readied himself to try again.

"Wait, let me try," said Max. He grabbed one of Ren's many screwdrivers and moved over to the robot, dropping to the floor as it swerved towards him. As he stood up, the robot swung an arm out; Max ducked just in time for it to miss his head, but there was a metallic clank as his sunglasses clattered to the ground.

"Oh, now you've made me mad!" Max told the robot. He ducked another punching arm

and jammed the screwdriver into the robot's power control with a shower of sparks. The robot jolted upright for a moment and then collapsed to the floor.

"You short-circuited it," said Alek with admiration.

"I just gave it a bit of a shock," laughed Max as he placed his sunglasses back on his head.

"Is everyone okay?" asked Ren Nagano, getting out of his special suit and running over to the RBI agents. "I've never known it do that before. I just can't think what caused the robot to behave that way!"

Max and Alek both looked at Zia.

"I think it might have been me," admitted Zia, sheepishly. She explained to Ren about her magnetism.

"Of course," he said, understanding. "Magnetic fields would affect the technology built into the suit."

"I know," nodded Max. "I try not to let Zia

anywhere near my inventions."

The agents agreed to come back the next day when Ren had rebooted his robot, to see it in action once more – and this time Zia would stay out of the way!

Max, Alek and Zia headed back to the area where they had spoken to the dragon witnesses. They sat on the sea wall that separated the little row of shops and restaurants from the beach area, and waited.

"I hope that dragon turns up soon," said Max, clearly bored.

As if on cue, the three agents heard screaming.

"It's coming from over there," said Alek, pointing to a car park and wide stretch of sand a little way along the beachfront. They could see a cloud of mist rolling steadily up the street.

"Then let's go," said Max, starting to run

towards the sound of the terrified people and the screeching of twisting metal. The others started after him.

The area was still thick with fog, but the agents were too late; they were met by the sight of crushed cars, the seawall broken in

several places and everything around them smoking, as if it had been singed by some sort of amazing heat source. But there was no sign of the dragon. Though the agents looked, it appeared that the creature had, once again, disappeared back into the sea, leaving only a trail of destruction in its wake.

A Concealed Clue

The following morning, the agents returned to Ren Nagano's scrapyard so he could give them another look at his new invention. Zia stayed in his workshop so that her magnetic energy wouldn't affect the demonstration. She looked around the room at all the parts: spare robot arms hung loosely from shelves, strange metallic creatures sat half-finished on tables, and motors from speedboats and motorcycles were all over the floor. There was every type of material you could ever want to build a robot from.

Dr Maxwell would love it here, she thought. Then, on one of the shelves, Zia noticed something familiar. It was a red and yellow tin with ornate writing on it, exactly like the one they had found before containing the letter from Robert Ripley about the quest to find his hidden artefacts.

Outside, Max and Alek were impressed as Ren's robot danced around, mimicking his movements faultlessly.

"I really like the robot," Max said to Alek, as Ren got his creation to break-dance for them, "and the control suit is a good idea, but I don't think we can include it in the database."

"But it's awesome," said Alek.

"I know," agreed Max. "I'll check with RIPLEY, but I'm sure this technology has been seen before."

"Ren will be so disappointed," said Alek, as he started to cough. "What's going on? I can hardly see him now."

Max too was having difficulty seeing the robot's latest dance move, due to the smoke now surrounding them.

"The robot must be fuelled like a car," explained Max. "There was a pipe attached to the back of the robot – I suppose that was its exhaust."

Ren came over to them, spluttering from the smog.

"I'm sorry," he said. "The robot runs on gasoline and it gets a little smoky if it has been on for a while. I've been looking at ways to make it safer. The mix I'm using now might make you cough, but it won't cause you any harm; but

>> In San Francisco they are hoping to harness the power of the horrible, smelly methane gas in dog poo so it can be used for heating homes and providing electricity. The method has already been tried with cows' poo and now experts want to create power from all kinds of manure, sewerage and household garbage.

I really do need to find some greener fuels."

"I can suggest a few," said Max eagerly, as the three of them went back into Ren's workshop. "Chocolate has been used to power cars and trucks. And there's a German guy who says he can make diesel out of dead cats!"

"Lovely," said Zia.

Ren laughed. "Well Zia, what do you make of my workshop? Hopefully it's more to your liking than dead-cat diesel?"

"It's really cool," she replied. "You've got everything here! But what is that?" She pointed to the red and yellow tin.

"Ah, that was my father's," Ren explained. "He called it his 'lucky tin'. An American man who visited many years ago gave it to him. My father was an inventor, too."

The RBI agents all looked at each other, wondering if that American visitor was the founder of Ripley High and the inspiration behind the Ripley's database.

Alek pulled out his R-phone and called up a picture of RIPLEY; the hologram had been designed to look like 'Rip'. He showed the R-phone to Ren.

"Did he look like this?" he asked.

"It was so long ago," Ren said, studying the picture. "But he does look quite familiar."

"What's in the tin?" asked Zia. "Can we see it?"

"Of course," Ren told her, reaching for the tin and opening it. "It's just an old luggage label from somewhere in America. I suppose that man must have had it on his suitcase and left it behind. Dad just kept them together."

Zia picked up the luggage label. It was from a hotel called the 'Little America Hotel' in Wyoming, USA. There was a note to hold the

bag for room 8 for the night of 26th May 1935 and a little logo of a penguin on the tag.

"Ooh, wasn't there a penguin in the photo Rip left us?" asked Zia. "I wonder if it's linked to that? It could be another clue!"

"I think it might be," said Alek, turning the label over in his hands. "So far, all the clues we've found have been in tins like this one. I just wonder what they all mean."

"Well, we haven't got time to think about it now, I'm afraid," said Max. "It's almost sunset and we need to make sure that we don't miss the dragon again!"

7

Metal Monster

The RBI agents decided to split up. Since the dragon had been seen in two different locations, they needed someone in both places. Alek went to the beach, where the dragon had appeared the night before, while Max and Zia went back to the little row of shops where most of the dragon sightings had been.

"Ha ha, look what it's doing!" Max laughed. To pass the time, he had brought a small robot with him. Normally, it just walked along, but Max was powering it up and holding it next to Zia. The robot would then jump and spin uncontrollably.

"You're mean," Zia told him, but with a smile; the little robot's antics were quite funny.

"Aw, you know I love you really, Z," he said.

"Wait, what's that?" she asked, jumping up.

A fog had started to gather in the distance on the beach – in the area where Alek was!

"Quick, we have to go over there," said Max, putting the little robot back into his pocket and then rapidly scanning the area around them. Leaning up against a wall was a police scooter with a storage compartment on the back and a helmet swinging from its handlebars. Max grabbed the helmet and pulled it on. He flicked the storage compartment open and threw the spare helmet that was in there to Zia.

"Put this on and jump on the back," he instructed her. Zia did as she was told and climbed on behind Max. Max quickly opened the bike's control panel, and after pressing a few buttons and swapping a few wires the scooter whirred into life. Soon, the pair were racing along the beachfront.

"Max, this is wrong," yelled Zia. She glanced behind her and noticed the policeman standing where his scooter had been, calling after them and waving his hands. "We've stolen that policeman's bike."

"Nah, we're just borrowing it," said Max, rebellious as ever. "I'll return it when we're done. Besides, hopefully the police will chase us."

"What?" asked Zia in amazement. "Then we'd be in big trouble!"

"Not once the cops see what we're up against," Max explained. "We could probably use their help with the dragon."

Meanwhile, Alek had also noticed the sea

mist gathering around him. The air began to grow warm and dry, as if a fire was raging nearby. Slowly two glowing red orbs appeared, burning their way through the mist as if seeking out their target. The heat intensified and as a burst of warmth washed over him Alek realised that the dragon was breathing fire! He checked that his fireproof vest was strapped on securely and, after taking a deep breath, headed into the fog towards the dragon.

As he got close to it, the dragon changed direction sharply, and disappeared further into the mist. Alek charged after the creature, but it was difficult to see anything through the thick smog. A woman's scream sounded somewhere and Alek turned on the hand-held sonar, pointing it in the direction of the scream. The display filled with little dots, showing what Alek decided were lots of people, and something else that looked enormous and its heat-signature was telling him that it was metallic.

The object seemed to be moving towards him, but before Alek could stop to think about it he saw the blazing red eyes of the dragon ahead of him. As he got closer the eyes began to flash, as if warning him away, but Alek continued. A huge three-toed foot thudded down in front of him and he had to jump backwards to avoid being squashed. As he looked at it, he realised that the mammoth foot was made of metal – the dragon must have been what was showing up on the sonar reader! Alek darted back again as a second metallic foot appeared and the rest of the creature pulled itself towards him. It was almost on top of him before recognition dawned; Alek suddenly had a thought about what this might be. It was the dragon sculpture from Ren Nagano's scrapyard! He had only seen it under the dust cover, but it was about the same size and shape. Alek couldn't understand it; somehow, it was now animated and moving – moving straight towards him!

The giant feet slammed down once more, forcing Alek to leap out of the way. He suddenly realised that the creature was trying to stomp on him and he tried to think of a plan; he wouldn't be able to get to his R-phone to alert the others and he kept dodging the metal monster. Besides, he thought, the others were all the way over the other side of the beach. Alek remembered how long it had taken them to get to the scene the night before; even if he could get the others here, they might not be in time to help him!

Gulping hard at the thought that he might end up squashed flat under the gigantic feet, Alek remembered all the poor snails and bugs he had accidentally stepped on in the past, and decided that he was not going to share their fate!

Alek set his feet firmly and squared up to the monster. Using his enormous strength, he tried to push the creature back. He was amazed at the power he felt surging towards him; the dragon was harder to move than the trucks he pulled in his strongman training. Pushing against the metal monster, he found himself starting to sweat; he couldn't remember the last time he had needed to exert such effort.

The more he pushed, the more the dragon pushed back.

Alek started to feel his strength draining and his feet beginning to slide backwards along the sand; he tried stepping forward, in a desperate attempt to hold his footing and to stop the huge metal mammoth from closing in on him, but it was no good – the monster was too strong for even him!

8

Short Circuits

Max and Zia arrived at the beach on their scooter.

"Oh, no!" cried Zia. "Alek!" She pointed to where he was using his contortionist ability to keep his footing. His body was twisting into weird shapes, his legs so far apart that he was almost doing the splits and his back arched as his hands struggled to keep pushing against the dragon.

"Get ready for a rough landing," said Max. Without slowing, he turned the scooter sharply and it skidded to a halt, sparks flying as it scraped along the concrete path and then beached itself in the sand.

"It's Ren's statue!" gasped Max, peering through the fog and instantly recognising the huge metal sculpture.

"It can't be," said Zia. "Statues don't move."

"Well, this one sure does!" said Max.

Dusting herself off, Zia rushed over to Alek. She moved as close as she dared to the dragon, hoping that her magnetism would affect it, but nothing happened. Confused, she moved closer and put her hands onto the cool metal of the creature's side. Again there was no change; the dragon just kept forcing Alek backwards.

Zia cried out in frustration, unsure of what to do.

"Go for the control panel," Max shouted to her. Zia remembered the way Max had stopped the robot in Ren's scrapyard. She raced towards the dragon and leaped at it, aiming her attack at its control panel. As she struck, volts of power surged through the creature's body. It shuddered, blue light flickering and crackling noises sounding all around, as something short-circuited within its body. Then the dragon stopped moving; the pressure it was applying on Alek stopped and its legs buckled. With an almighty crash, the statue crumpled to the sand, making the ground around it shudder. The red eyes began to dim, until they shrank to pin-size circles before dying completely.

"Phew," sighed Alek, heaving himself away from the metal carcass. "You two certainly left your rescue till the last minute."

"Nah," said Max. "We knew we'd be here in the nick of time."

Zia, Alek noticed, did not look so sure.

"So what exactly happened?" she asked. "Is this Ren's statue?"

"I'd say so," Max told her.

"It definitely is," said Alek. "I got a pretty good look at it."

"But statues don't move!" Zia argued.

"I think Ren told us a little fib," said Max. "I

don't think this is a statue at all. I think it's an advanced robotic prototype."

"You don't think Ren is trying to hurt us, do you?" asked Zia.

"Perhaps he heard us saying that we didn't think his robot was good enough to be included in the database," suggested Alek.

"Maybe," Max said thoughtfully, "but I just don't see Ren as the violent type. I think this robot has got out of control all by itself."

"But if it's a robot," Zia began, "why did it not react to me? Ren's suit went crazy when I was near it."

"I don't know," admitted Max. "Maybe it's just too big."

A loud creak came from the pile of metal and the eyes flashed back on. Slowly, the creature began to move, the long body rising steadily up on to its short legs; one of the enormous feet stood forward on its three toes.

"This isn't good," Alek murmured.

"What do we do?" asked Zia, panic in her voice.

"Run?" suggested Alek, moving away from the dragon. Max and Zia followed, but too quickly. In their hurry to get away, they didn't look where they were going, crashed into each other and fell to the ground in a heap.

Flames shot out of the dragon's nostrils as it approached the pair of RBI agents struggling to get up.

"Zia, hurry!" shouted Max as he tried to stand, but now he was panicking and his feet kept slipping on the sand.

"I can't!" cried Zia, as her own feet lost their grip. The approaching metal monster was now almost on top of them; the heat from its fire was almost unbearable. Alek quickly turned back, realising he was going to have to do something remarkable to get the other agents out of trouble.

The dragon's foot rose into the air, ready to

slam down on the trapped pair. Alek used the sea wall to help him: he jumped up on to it and then backflipped over the dragon's foot, grabbing Max and Zia as he passed them. They flew through the air with him until all three landed safely to the side of the dragon. It swung its head towards the prey that had escaped it, and began moving towards them once more.

"How did it recover so quickly?" asked Max. "I short-circuited it pretty good." They

quickly ran to a safe distance away from the recovering robot.

"Maybe it runs on some weird energy source?" suggested Zia, "and that energy makes it restart if its system shuts down. I've heard of things like that."

"Or maybe it's because there's a DUL agent in a suit controlling it," said Alek.

"It's something DUL might do," said Max.

"No, silly," protested Alek. "Look! There's

a DUL agent in a suit like Ren's, controlling the dragon."

The other two looked to where Alek was pointing and saw what he meant. Through the haze, the RBI agents could make out a pair of DUL agents in their uniform of black suits and shiny shoes. Only one of the agents had accessorised his DUL outfit with a robotic suit – very similar to the one that Ren Nagano had worn to control his robot.

9

Remote-control Robot

"So the dragon is really a robot?" asked Zia.

"That explains a lot," said Max. "Ren must have created it to work in the same way as the one he showed us."

"But why didn't he tell us about it?" asked Alek.

"I'm not sure," Max admitted. "Perhaps he wasn't ready to share his latest creation with us yet? Sometimes I don't really like people to see what I'm working on until it's ready. It gives me time to make sure that it works first."

"Or maybe Ren suspected that it was his robot that was causing all the attacks, but didn't want to have to face it?" said Zia. "I'd be a little worried about letting everyone know if I thought that something that big was my fault."

"The mist must be the smoke from the exhaust," said Alek suddenly. "Remember the way the fumes choked us at the scrapyard? And this robot is so much bigger that it must use a lot more fuel."

"But we're not choking now," said Max suddenly aware of his easy breathing. "Ren told us that he was trying new sorts of fuel for his creations and that the mix he used for the robot at his scrapyard might make you cough but wouldn't harm you – this must be an even more advanced version that doesn't even make you cough. That's a pretty amazing thing." Max was obviously impressed. "The DUL agents must have got their hands on the most recent fuel."

"That's all very well," said Zia, bringing the conversation back to their task in hand. "But what can we do to stop the dragon? My ability only stopped it for a moment, Max's idea of short-circuiting it only stopped it for a moment and Alek, not even you can stop something like this."

"We need to go after the DUL agent controlling the dragon," decided Max. "If we stop the DUL agents the dragon will just be a harmless robot again."

Alek and Zia nodded in agreement at Max's idea and then the three RBI agents made a run for the DUL agents. As they did the robotic dragon cut right across their path. They changed direction, sharply doubling back to appear behind where the dragon was, but the robot swiftly changed course too and was in front of them in an instant.

"This is no good," complained Zia. "Everywhere we go the DUL agents just send the dragon to stop us."

"Let's split up," suggested Max. "Alek and I will keep the dragon occupied and Zia, you try to sneak through to the DUL agent in the suit."

"Wouldn't Alek be more likely to stop him?" asked Zia as she twisted around to escape the dragon, only to find it straight back on her heels.

"I'm hoping that your ability will work," Max told her, panting as he also jumped out of the dragon's path.

"Max is right," said Alek, quickly backflipping out of the raging robot's path. "The dragon might be too big, but the suit is the same size as Ren's and your ability worked on his. If they can't control the robot then we have a chance to stop them."

"And quickly, please," said Max. "I'm getting quite exhausted here!"

"Okay ..." said Zia, a little unsure.

Alek ran at the robot, knocking its head from side to side, so that fire shot out across the empty beach. Max leaped on to the dragon's back and began seeing if he could hack into its source of power. Zia watched until she was sure that the attention of the DUL agents was on them and then darted through its legs. She shimmied along on the ground under the dragon, being careful not to hit her head on its metallic body. She pulled herself out from under the creature's tail and searched for the DUL agents, only to see them right in front of her. The agent in the suit was jerking wildly.

"What's going on?" he asked his partner. "I've lost control of the robot! It's like it's controlling me now!"

Zia smiled to herself; this is what they were hoping would happen. Because she was so close, the DUL agent was no longer able to direct the dragon's attack.

Suddenly, there was a loud crash that sounded as if the brick wall had exploded. Zia whipped her head around and saw the dragon weaving uncontrollably. Its tail had smashed against the wall, sending brick and concrete in all different directions. She squinted through the mist and saw Max clinging desperately to the writhing tail, bracing himself for a second impact with the unforgiving wall.

Her eyes widened with panic – she was disrupting the DUL agent's control of the dragon, but she still couldn't stop the dragon itself.

Alek ran towards Zia and threw himself at the DUL agent in the suit, tackling him to the ground. The DUL agent fell and hit the sand, but moved far enough away from Zia for him, once again, to get the robot to move to his will.

The second DUL agent ran away, screaming as huge flames seared through the air as the dragon began to move towards Alek. Zia ran over to where he had the DUL agent pinned down and the robot reverted to manic, jerky movements as its signal was interrupted by her magnetism.

"I ... can't ... hold him ... down ... forever," said Alek, struggling.

"Get him to the water," yelled Max, appearing beside them, having won his battle with the dragon's tail. The DUL agent broke free from Alek's grasp and scrambled to his feet.

Immediately, Alek started running after him, making sure that he was directing the robotic-suited DUL agent towards the sea. The

DUL agent, thinking he was escaping from his RBI pursuer, was only too happy to run in the direction he was being chased. Realising that the salt water probably wouldn't be any good for the robotic suit, he stopped suddenly on the water line. He took an uncertain step back and immediately regretted it. The sand by the water was softer than the tightly packed sand elsewhere on the beach, and it collapsed easily under the weight of the DUL agent's metal-encased foot. Alek stopped just short of the water and watched the amusing spectacle of the DUL agent trying to keep his balance; his arms waved wildly out at his sides, as if he was swinging a skipping rope. His whole body wobbled from left to right, forwards and backwards, until gravity won and he plopped into the sea with a splash.

For a second, nothing happened. Then a blue spark flashed from the suit, followed by a larger crackle of energy, and then another, and another, until the whole suit lit up like a Christmas tree, before the light faded and the DUL agent was left wearing a metal suit that did nothing.

On the beach behind them, the huge metal dragon slumped to the sand. Its remote control had been severed and it was a statue again.

A Database Entry

"I'm so sorry," said Ren Nagano. The RBI agents had called the inventor and told him about their adventure on the beach. He had then arrived with his other suit and used it to walk the dragon back to his scrapyard. "I know I should have told you what Ryujin really was, but I didn't think he was ready."

Ren explained that he had built the Ryujin robot first, but it had been difficult to control;

and it had produced so much smoke so quickly that it had become very difficult to see almost as soon as he started using it. The inventor had thought that perhaps he could perfect the technology on a smaller scale and learn how to control his movements when wearing the suit. So that was why he had built the smaller robot

▶▶ Saya, a robotic teacher, has been developed to teach classes at a school in Tokyo. She has a range of expressions and can speak many languages, set tasks and even get angry when pupils fall out of line. She has brown hair, pink lipstick and has been designed to look as close to a human being as possible.

based on himself, as a test model. While he had been doing this he had also been working on a new, cleaner type of fuel for the dragon robot. This new fuel meant that people around didn't choke as soon as the robot started to work. He had found something that worked pretty well.

He was also almost there with controlling the movements of the Ren robot, but still hadn't tested the new fuel mix on it yet.

The DUL agents must have sneaked in and stolen the prototype of the suit that controlled Ryujin. Each night they must have taken Ryujin

out of the yard and used him to scare people, pretending to be the dragon from the myths. "If Ren hadn't finished his new cleaner fuel he would have probably heard them coughing their way out of the yard and been able to stop them!" said Max.

The RBI agents looked at each other. Stealing the robot to panic people into thinking a real dragon was terrorising Japan was the sort of thing DUL lived for. DUL agents were always trying to get a lie into the RBI database.

"What are you going to do now?" Max asked Ren.

"For a start, I'm going to make sure I have a better lock on my scrapyard," said Ren, "and speaking to you, Max, has given me lots of ideas for cleaner fuels to power my robots too. Hopefully, I will now be able to demonstrate them and my audience will actually be able to see my creations, not just the cloud of smoke they produce!"

"Environmentally friendly robots," said Max. "Now that really would be something for our database."

"So did my robot qualify?" asked Ren, eagerly.

"Yes and no," said Max. Ren looked confused.

"The first robot didn't," Max explained. "I'm afraid it's just not new enough technology. We've seen loads of things like that before."

Ren's face fell; he had so wanted to have his work entered into the Ripley database.

"However," Max continued, "a 12-metre dragon robot that breathes fire and crushes cars is certainly worth entering in the Ripley database!"

After celebrating with Ren, the agents left the scrapyard, ready for their homeward journey back to BION Island. They paused just outside Ren's scrapyard gates.

"You've got to hand it to DUL on this one," said Max.

"What do you mean?" asked Zia, shocked that Max was admiring DUL and their nasty tricks.

"Real, live, sea dragons would have been a great thing to have in the database," Max explained.

"But real dragons are pretty unbelievable," said Zia.

"Believe it or not, so are gymnasts strong enough to take on a giant metal dragon, and girls who can save the day by disrupting an infrared robotic control suit with their electro-magnetism!"

"You think I saved the day?" asked Zia. Max teased her so much about her ability that she was amazed to hear him say something complimentary.

"Well, if it wasn't for you and your ability, we would never have been able to stop that DUL agent sending Ryujin after us."

Zia's smile widened; she was happy that her

ability was useful.

"So does this mean I can help you with your robots now?" she asked.

"Whoah," said Max, holding his hand up to tell Zia that she had got carried away. "I don't think so. You might have been useful here, in Japan, but back on BION Island I want you and your magnetic vibes to stay well clear of me and my robots." He pulled his sunglasses down over his eyes and walked off.

"Never mind," said Alek, putting his arm around Zia, as two police scooters appeared around the corner. One of them looked very scratched and its rider was pointing at Max.

"He's the one who stole my bike," said the policeman.

"Hey, I returned it," Max protested.

"Oh, dear," said Zia to Alek. "It seems that Max's idea of 'borrowing' the scooter didn't go down as well as he thought it would."

"Especially as he ruined it before giving it

back," Alek pointed out. "I'll go and try to help. Zia, you call Mr Cain. I think we might need his diplomatic skills here!"

Zia sighed and pulled her R-phone out of her pocket to dial the number for RBI headquarters. It had certainly been an eventful trip to Japan!

RIPLEY'S DATABASE ENTRY

RIPLEY FILE NUMBER : 22696

MISSION BRIEF : Believe it or not. witnesses in Japan have reported being terrorised by a huge dragon on the coast of Japan. Investigate accuracy of these accounts and collect factual information for Ripley database.

CODE NAME : Sea Dragon

REAL NAME : Robo- Ryujin

LOCATION : Tokyo, Japan

AGE : n/a

HEIGHT : 12 m

WEIGHT : 27,215 kg

VIDEO CAPTURE

UNUSUAL CHARACTERISTICS :

Metal robot based on a Japanese dragon. Huge three-toed feet that can crush cars, glowing red eyes and a mouth that spits flames. The robot copies the movements of a person in a hi-tech body suit.

RBI DATABASE APPROVED!

INVESTIGATING AGENTS :

Max Johnson, Zia Mendoza, Alek Filipov

▶▶ YOUR NEXT ASSIGNMENT

115

JOIN THE RBI IN THEIR NEXT ADVENTURE!

RUNNING WILD

Prologue

10 years ago, somewhere over the border of western China

The small plane buzzed like an angry hornet as it wheeled round beneath the clouds searching for somewhere to land, a plume of white smoke streaming from one engine. Clearly, it was in trouble ...

Suddenly, the plane banked sharply to the

left, heading for a small clearing in the vast expanse of forest below. As it came in to land it was losing height fast. Too fast! Its wings clipped the tops of the giant conifers, crashing through their upper branches. Nose-first, it ploughed through the understorey towards the clearing. The ground shook as the fuselage slammed down on the forest floor and shot like a giant missile towards a narrow gap in the trees, gouging a deep scar in the earth. With a sickening crunch, the nose crumpled as it was forced between two trees, the wings shearing off on impact. At last, the plane stopped.

The silence that followed was deafening. Time passed, but it was impossible to say how long. Then as the light began to fade, from somewhere inside the wreckage came the thin wail of a young child. It was a little girl, no more than five or six years old. Partly buried beneath luggage bags, she cried out for help, but no one came.

Barely conscious, the little girl struggled to free herself. Crawling on all fours, she made her way towards a gaping hole in the side of the fuselage and looked out. Then she struggled to her feet, climbed out of the plane and stumbled into the darkening forest ...

ENTER THE STRANGE WORLD OF RIPLEY'S...

▶▶ Believe it or not, there is a lot of truth in this remarkable tale. The Ripley's team travels the globe to track down true stories that will amaze you. Read on to find out about real Ripley's case files and discover incredible facts about some of the extraordinary people and places in our world.

Ripley's
Believe *It or Not!* ®

▶▶ ROBOSAURUS

Robosaurus is a giant mechanical dinosaur 12 metres high and seven times more powerful than a T-Rex dinosaur.

▶▶ Mechanical jaws have a crushing force of 9,000 kilos and grabbing claws are even stronger.

▶▶ Nostrils function as flamethrowers that spit 6-metre flames.

▶▶ Robosaurus is capable of lifting an entire jet airplane and tearing it in half.

▶▶ Robosaurus is hungry for metal and tears off car roofs and doors with its 130-centimetre steel teeth.

credit: TSGT Joe Zuccaro/AP/PA Photos

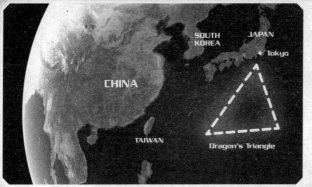

credit: © JLV Image Works–Fotolia.com

SOUTH KOREA

JAPAN

Tokyo

CHINA

TAIWAN

Dragon's Triangle

▶▶ The Dragon's Triangle is an area of the Pacific between Tokyo and Taiwan where boats have mysteriously disappeared.

▶▶ A number of Japanese boats vanished without trace inside the Dragon's Triangle in the 1950s.

▶▶ The Dragon's Triangle is similar to the mysterious Bermuda Triangle, with deep holes and strong volcanic activity that means whole islands can appear and disappear very quickly.

▶▶ Sailor Frederik Fransson was close to the Dragon's Triangle near Tonga and Fiji when he witnessed the birth of an island on his boat as it sailed through the pumice stone that rose from the sea.

▶▶ This area is home to the Mariana Trench, which at nearly 11 kilometres down is the deepest known place on Earth – deeper than Mount Everest, the world's highest mountain, is high.

▶▶ It is estimated that there are 30,000 islands in the Pacific Ocean.

>> The name 'Lucky Dragon' comes from a boat contaminated by a nuclear bomb in the 1950s.

▶▶ LUCKY DRAGON

credit: Reiko Tsukamasa/Rex Features

Japanese artist Kenji Yanobe created a 15-metre-long animatronic fire-breathing dragon boat in 2009, called 'Lucky Dragon'.

▶▶ It is half-dragon, half-boat, and can really flap its wings.

▶▶ The dragon's neck can extend 7 metres above the water.

▶▶ The dragon spits flames and water and has glowing red eyes.

▶▶ David Hanson's robot is able to copy 28 facial movements including smiling, sneering, frowning and arched eyebrows.

▶▶ Big Rig Jig is a sculpture made from two 18-wheeler trucks joined together rising four stories into the air.

Robots

credit: Courtesy of David Hanson

▶▶ Olesio da Silva from Brazil made a full-size robocar that can transform from a regular minivan to a 3.5-metre robot.

▶▶ Japanese scientists have developed a dancing robot that can follow a human dancer's lead. It predicts the dancer's next move through hand pressure applied to its back.

▶▶ Artist Christian Ristow and a team of builders created a giant mechanical crushing hand out of scrap metal in 2007. It is 8 metres long and weighs 2250 kilogrammes. The machine moves just like a human hand and can easily lift and crush entire vehicles.

▶▶ ROBOT CLONE

Zou Ren Ti from China created a remarkably life-like robot replica of himself, called Zou Ren Ti 2!

▶▶ Zou Ren Ti used to make figures for museums, but realised they would be even more realistic if he made them into robots.

▶▶ The cloned robot can move its face and talk just like Zou.

▶▶ Zou Ren Ti 2 has ultra-realistic skin made from a silica gel.

credit: Reuters/Jason Lee

▶▶ It is almost impossible to distinguish the robot man from the human (the real Zou Ren Ti is on the left!).

▶▶ In his lifetime, Ripley travelled over 720,000 kilometres looking for oddities – the distance from Earth to the Moon and back again.

▶▶ Ripley had a large collection of cars, but he couldn't drive. He also bought a Chinese sailing boat, called Mon Lei, but he couldn't swim.

▶▶ Ripley was so popular that his weekly mailbag often exceeded 170,000 letters, all full of weird and wacky suggestions for his cartoon strip.

▶▶ He kept a boa constrictor 8.5 metres long as a pet in his New York home.

▶▶ Ripley's Believe It or Not! cartoon is the longest-running cartoon strip in the world, read in 42 countries and 17 languages every day.

In 1918, Robert Ripley became fascinated by strange facts while he was working as a cartoonist at the *New York Globe*. He was passionate about travel and, by 1940, had visited no less than 201 countries, gathering artefacts and searching for stories that would be right for his column, which he named Believe It or Not!

Ripley bought an island estate at Mamaroneck, New York, and filled the huge house there with unusual objects and odd creatures that he'd collected on his explorations.

PACKED WITH FUN & GAMES, THE **RBI** WEBSITE IS HERE! CHECK IT OUT

REVIEWS

DOWNLOADS

MAPS & DATA

MORE TEAM TALK

THE NEXT FILES